RIDES THE WAVES

BY **KARA WEST**   ILLUSTRATED BY **LEEZA HERNANDEZ**

LITTLE SIMON
New York London Toronto Sydney New Delhi

LITTLE SIMON

An imprint of Simon & Schuster Children's Publishing Division

1230 Avenue of the Americas, New York, New York 10020

First Little Simon hardcover edition June 2021

Copyright © 2021 by Simon & Schuster, Inc.

Also available in a Little Simon paperback edition

All rights reserved, including the right of reproduction in whole or in part in any form.

LITTLE SIMON is a registered trademark of Simon & Schuster, Inc., and associated colophon is a trademark of Simon & Schuster, Inc.

For information about special discounts for bulk purchases, please contact Simon & Schuster Special Sales at 1-866-506-1949 or business@simonandschuster.com.

The Simon & Schuster Speakers Bureau can bring authors to your live event.

For more information or to book an event contact the Simon & Schuster Speakers Bureau at 1-866-248-3049 or visit our website at www.simonspeakers.com.

Designed by Laura Roode

Manufactured in the United States of America 0421 FFG

2 4 6 8 10 9 7 5 3 1

Library of Congress Cataloging-in-Publication Data

Names: West, Kara, author. | Hernandez, Leeza, illustrator.

Title: Mia Mayhem rides the waves / by Kara West ; illustrated by Leeza Hernandez.

Description: First Little Simon paperback edition. | New York : Little Simon, 2021. | Series: Mia Mayhem ; [11] | Summary: Mia Mayhem learns some important things about herself and her abilities during a family vacation to the beach.

Identifiers: LCCN 2020050437 (print) | LCCN 2020050438 (eBook) | ISBN 9781534484429 (paperback) | ISBN 9781534484436 (hardcover) | ISBN 9781534484443 (eBook)

Subjects: CYAC: Vacations—Fiction. | Beaches—Fiction. | Family life—Fiction. | Abililty—Fiction. | Superheroes—Fiction. | African Americans—Fiction.

Classification: LCC PZ7.1.W43684 Mn 2021 (print) | LCC PZ7.1.W43684 (eBook) | DDC [Fic]—dc23

LC record available at https://lccn.loc.gov/2020050437

LC eBook record available at https://lccn.loc.gov/2020050438

CONTENTS

CHAPTER 1   VACATION TIME!   1

CHAPTER 2   THE BEACH BUM   13

CHAPTER 3   THE SURFING LESSON   21

CHAPTER 4   A TRASHED BEACH!   33

CHAPTER 5   SEAGULLS ON PATROL   43

CHAPTER 6   MAYHEM ON THE BEACH   55

CHAPTER 7   BOARDWALK FUN   69

CHAPTER 8   A NEW FRIEND   81

CHAPTER 9   SAND SCULPTURES   95

CHAPTER 10   THE PERFECT VACATION   109

VACATION TIME!

"Finally! I found it!" I cheered. I stood on top of my bed, holding my wet suit up as if I had just won a trophy.

I'd emptied every drawer and turned my closet inside out trying to find it. And all this time it was right on top of my T-shirt pile! I looked around my room in shock. It looked like a tornado had just passed through.

But luckily, it's times like these when being a superhero comes in handy.

Yeah, you heard me right.

My name is Mia Macarooney, and *I. Am. A. Superhero!* Like, for real!

My life gets pretty messy sometimes, but no matter how bad things get, I can always clean things up in a flash.

Here, let me show you.

See?

My room looks as good as new, and now, finally, I'm one step closer to . . . vacation!

I've been waiting for this day *for a long time*. I'm so ready that I could burst!

You see, this superhero life gets really busy, really fast.

There's so much to juggle all the time. During normal school hours, my

classmates know me as Mia Macarooney. But after regular school ends, I race over to the Program for In Training Superheroes, aka the PITS! The PITS is a top secret superhero training academy where I learn everything I need to know about being super.

And I wouldn't want things any other way. My life is pretty awesome.

But honestly? It *does* get really tiring sometimes.

So that's why my parents decided it was time to go on an epic family beach vacation!

I happily sank down onto my bed
when a loud screech made me jump.

"MEOW!"

"Oops! Sorry, Chaos!" I cried. I'd
rolled over my cat's paw by mistake. I
could tell by the big grumpy look on
her face that she was *not* happy.

"Hey, girl, I'm really sorry you can't come," I said. "But the hotel doesn't allow pets. And anyway, you'll have plenty of fun at Eddie's!"

Right away, she perked up and walked right into her carrier, ready to go. Eddie is my best friend, and he's got a friendly dog named Pax, who is best buddies with my grumpy old cat.

I jumped off my bed and threw my wet suit into my suitcase. Then I clicked it shut and ran downstairs at the speed of light.

"Ah, just in time, Mia!" my mom exclaimed. The car was so jam-packed that there was barely any room for us! We had to pack surfboards, boogie boards, a beach tent, sandcastle buckets, towels, and of course, a cooler full of snacks.

SUPER 1

Now, you might be wondering why we're driving to the beach. Isn't flying much faster?

Yes, of course it is!

But when you're a superhero, you have to protect your secret identity, which means we do *a lot* of things the superordinary way.

So that's why we all piled into our packed car, dropped Chaos off at Eddie's, and then got ready for a long three-hour drive.

THE BEACH BUM

After a bunch of car games and several catnaps, we finally arrived at our hotel, the Beach Bum. I broke into a big smile as we drove into the parking lot. It was the perfect beach getaway.

We grabbed all our bags at once and rushed to the check-in counter. If the outside looked this cool, I knew our room was going to be amazing.

And I was totally right. I mean, look at this place!

The room was decorated with octopus and jellyfish everywhere! There was an octopus-shaped lamp, starfish-shaped pillows, and even jellyfish-patterned blankets! I picked my bed and jumped onto it. Sleeping away from home was going to be so much fun!

"Wow! Look at this view!" Dad exclaimed as he pulled back the starfish curtains.

"Come on—let's go catch some waves!" I yelled as I pressed my nose up to the window.

I quick-changed into my wet suit and zipped to the door when my dad stopped me.

"Hold on, Mia," he said. "We need your help with this beach gear!"

We had so much stuff that you'd have thought we were camping for days! I grabbed my surfboard, sandcastle toys, and towels while my parents grabbed

the chairs, tent, and cooler. Normally, I would have carried everything by myself, no problem. But at the beach, we didn't want to stand out too much.

And luckily, when we got down to the water, no one else was in sight, so we found the best spot and used our superspeed to set up.

Then came the not-so-fun part: putting on sunscreen. I hate the sticky feeling of it. But getting a sunburn is no fun (I learned that the hard way), so I shut my eyes and wiggled around as my mom rubbed sunscreen all over my face.

When I opened my eyes, I was finally ready! So I grabbed my yellow surfboard and ran into the rushing waves.

CHAPTER 3

THE SURFING LESSON

"Ah, it's so cold!" I yelled out happily. The water hadn't warmed up yet, but I was so excited to go surfing that I didn't care. My parents and I haven't gone surfing in a long time, so I was worried I'd be a little rusty. But as soon as I saw the first wave, I knew what I needed to do.

I watched carefully as the wave got bigger and bigger.

Then I lay down on my stomach and started lifting my knee to stand . . . until my right foot slipped and I tumbled into the water! I swam toward the surface as fast as I could. When I popped my head up for air, I spotted my dad riding the end of an epic wave. My dad has always loved the water and was a surfing pro.

But not me—I used to hate the water because waves looked like big monster arms! But one summer my dad took me to the pool every day to teach me how to swim. It wasn't easy at first, but soon I realized that being in the water wasn't so bad. And now I'm a pretty good swimmer.

Well, not as good as my dad, obviously. But I can work on that.

As I got back on my board, my dad swam over.

"Hey, Mia, remember to use your core strength to balance your weight. Just like when you fly in the air. It'll help you stay steady!"

I smiled and gave him a nod as we waited for another wave. And this time, I did it! I rode the wave all the way to its end and then splashed down into clear, shallow water.

Victory! I gave my dad a big high five.

Now that I was getting the hang of it, it was time to have some fun. With each big wave, I got more and more steady. I loved riding the waves side by side with my dad. There couldn't be anything better than this, and I wanted to stay all day long.

SPLASH!

But of course, my mom had other plans.

"Hey, Mia! Hey, honey! Come back to the tent!" I heard my mom call. Even

HEY, MIA!

with the waves crashing around us, we could hear her voice crystal clear.

Ever since I got my superpowers, my five senses have sharpened. And I have to say, in times like this, super-hearing comes in handy. But it's not so fun in the bathroom at school, if you know what I mean.

PEE-YEW!

My dad and I rode one more big wave on our way toward the shore.

As I was walking out of the water, I felt something tugging at my board. At first I thought it was just a slimy piece of seaweed. But when I looked closer, it was a piece of trash!

I pulled the plastic bag off my board and scrunched it in my hand. I was so relieved that I caught it before it floated away. But then I looked up, and my mouth dropped open.

Now that it was low tide, there was trash scattered everywhere!

And if I didn't do something fast, there was a swarm of seagulls in front of me that were waiting to do some serious damage.

A TRASHED BEACH!

Most people at the beach would avoid running into a swarm of birds. That would be the smart—or I guess, normal—thing to do.

But I'm not like most people, so I ran right into the middle of the squawking birds, flapping my arms as if I had wings. It might have looked weird . . . but it worked! All their eyes were on me.

"Sorry to bother you, but listen—that is not food!" I cried out to the flock of seagulls. "It'll make you sick!"

Now, let me pause here.

Are you asking yourself if I'm really talking to these seagulls?

Yes, yes I am indeed.

Talking to animals is a superpower I've been learning how to control at the PITS. Some animals are easier to talk to than others. And it turns out that seagulls are not easy to talk to—at all.

No matter what I said or did, they were not interested.

But I didn't want them to eat the trash, so I scooped up the garbage with the bag I'd found in the water. Then I ran to my parents as fast as I could.

"Mom! Dad!" I cried in a huff. "The seagulls were trying to eat this trash!"

"Oh, that's awful!" my mom replied with a frown.

"But this isn't all of it!" I said, waving toward the beach. "There's garbage scattered everywhere!"

My dad had a very serious look on his face.

"Mia, we need to keep this beach clean and safe for the animals," he said. "But it's not only about the animals, either—our trash hurts our environment, too."

This was the first time I'd ever seen my dad so serious.

When we first arrived at the beach, I thought this vacation was going to be relaxing with lots of surfing, some reading, and sandcastle building. But seeing my dad so worried, I knew right away that there was only one thing to do.

"Let's do a beach cleanup!" I yelled out.

"Oh, great idea, Mia! I packed disposable gloves in the beach bag just in case," my mom replied.

I smiled big. I could always count on my mom to be ready for any situation.

"Great. We can use my sandcastle buckets to carry trash!" I said.

With our gloves, buckets, and shovels, we were ready to get our hands dirty.

It was time for the Macarooney family to save the beach!

CHAPTER 5

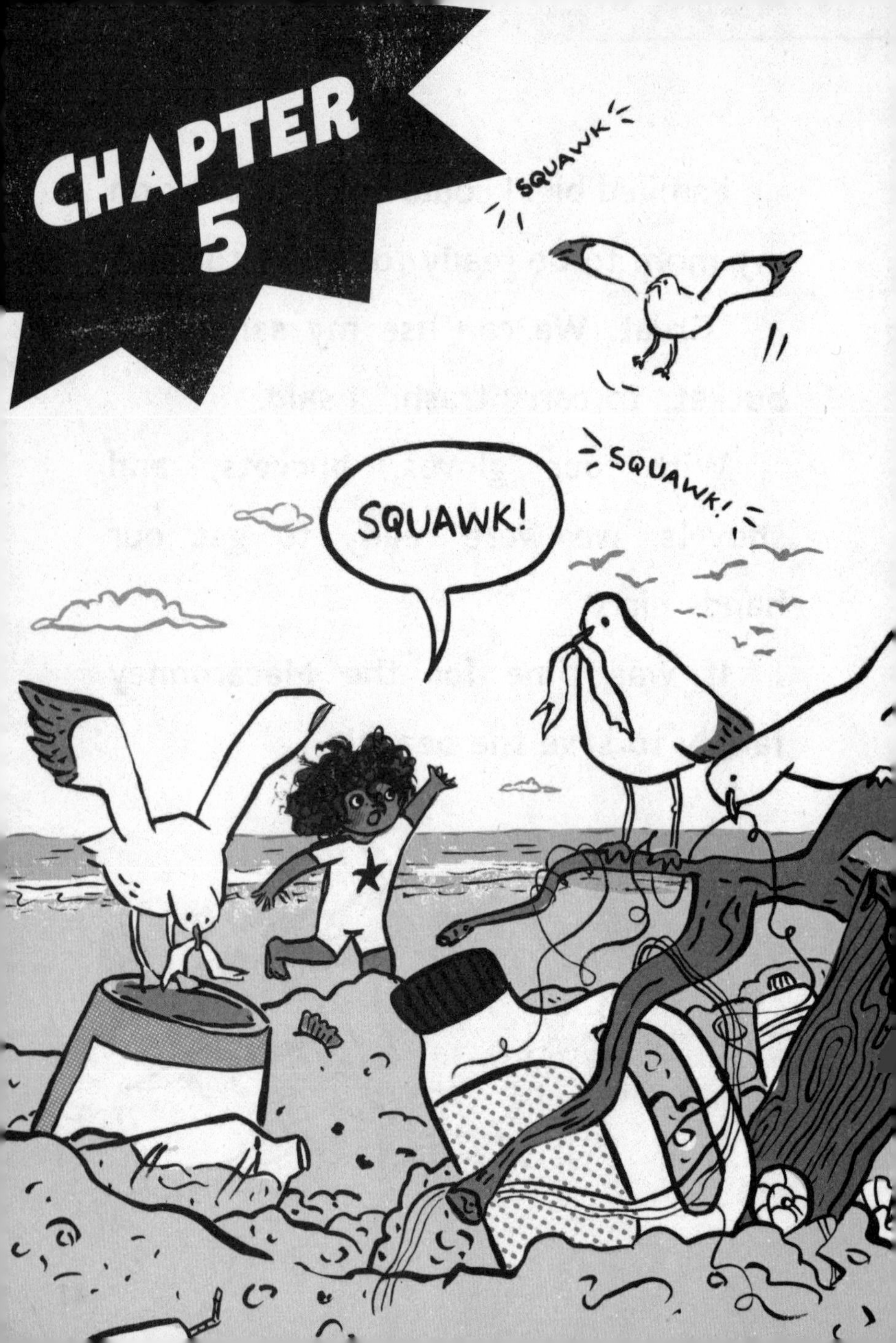

SEAGULLS ON PATROL

When I ran back toward the seagulls, they had already moved on to another pile of garbage. I tried to shoo them away, but this time, I swear, one of them gave me the stink eye.

I used to be scared of seagulls and anything else that could fly.

But that all changed when I learned to fly myself!

Once I realized that seagulls and I had something in common, they weren't so scary anymore.

I looked up at the sky and wished I could soar through the air like them right now.

Then I could fly around and pick up all the trash in no time!

In fact, I have so many powers that would come in handy.

With superstrength, I could look under all the rocks at once. And if I could use superspeed, this whole beach would be clean in minutes!

But right now, I needed to find a solution as regular Mia.

I was thinking as hard as I could when a seagull swooped down and grabbed my shovel.

"Hey! That's it!" I yelled.

My parents and I might not have been able to use our obvious powers, but my dad and I *could* talk to the animals.

"Hey, Dad!" I called excitedly. "Since the seagulls are good at finding the garbage, why don't we work together?"

Dad's face lit up right away. "Of course! That's a great idea, Mia. Animals are the best helpers."

My dad was the best at seagull talk,
so my mom and I put him to the task.
I couldn't hear him, but the seagull he
was talking to looked him straight in
the eye and nodded back.

Then a few seconds later, the seagull swooped back to the rest of its friends!

I watched with awe as they got to work right away. We hadn't trained them, but they knew what to do. As I watched one bird find a piece of trash and dump it into a bucket, I knew we were going to be a great team!

We started walking along the shore
in single file, looking for more garbage,
when I saw a girl with a huge sandcastle.
She must have spent all morning on it!

Before I could even stop it, the seagull right behind me swooped in . . . and knocked down a tower from the girl's sandcastle!

WHOOSH!

Then the other birds swooped down
and destroyed the rest of it too!

In seconds, the amazing sandcastle
was just a pile of sand.

I stood frozen in place, not sure what to do, when the girl pointed at me and burst into tears.

MAYHEM ON THE BEACH

All I had wanted was a relaxing vacation. I just wanted to surf and have a good time with my parents.

But instead, I somehow caused total mayhem, as usual.

I had no idea why the seagulls were acting out. They were knocking down castles, umbrellas, and chairs, and even scaring some of the other kids!

I was looking around in a panic (even superheroes don't know what to do sometimes), when my dad came over with a lifeguard.

"Everyone, freeze!" my dad yelled at the top of his lungs.

Just like that, it worked! Even the seagulls stopped what they were doing.

"Wow, what happened here?" the lifeguard asked after my dad unfroze everyone. "I'm afraid we're going to have to close the beach for a few hours to fix things."

A loud groan echoed through the crowd.

And I just felt terrible. Was it all my fault?

I emptied my buckets into the garbage can, but even that didn't make me feel better.

This vacation was turning out to be a total bust.

I wished I could fast-forward through the rest of it and get back home to regular life.

"Mia, I know that didn't end as planned, but we can still have fun," my mom said with a smile. "Let's go get dinner."

I wasn't in the mood, but I had to admit that I was pretty hungry.

So we headed out to a restaurant called the Happy Crabber. Our table was shaped like a boat that we had to climb into, which normally would have made me laugh. But after a day like today, I just wanted to sink into my seat.

"Hey, Mia, look!" Dad exclaimed, holding up the menu. "They've got hush puppies!"

My dad knew that hush puppies were my absolute favorite.

But that night? Even a delicious plate of hush puppies couldn't make me feel better.

"Mia, I know things didn't end well, but we're still very proud of you," my mom said.

"Unexpected things happen all the time," my dad added. "Especially with animals."

I shrugged my shoulders and sighed.

"But if I was better at talking to animals, they would have listened!" I exclaimed.

"If that were true, then I never would have accidentally caused that gerbil stampede downtown last year!" my dad said with a laugh.

I looked up at my dad and smiled. If my dad had trouble too . . . I guess he had a point.

After a really good dinner, we got ice cream and then walked along the boardwalk while my dad told more crazy animal stories that cracked me up.

By the time we got back to the hotel, I was feeling a lot better and was ready to crash into my comfy bed.

BOARDWALK FUN

The next morning I opened my eyes
and jumped up in shock. There was an
octopus looking right at me.

Um . . . *what* was going on?

I rubbed my eyes and looked around.
It turned out to be my pillow!

After a good night's sleep, I was in a
way better mood. Maybe this vacation
had a chance after all!

"Want to hit the beach?" my mom asked as we got ready.

"Can we go to the boardwalk first?" I requested. After yesterday, I decided it was better to have a little break from the beach.

So that's exactly what we did.

We walked around and checked out all the games and rides.

"What's first?" Dad asked with a grin.

"The log ride!" Mom and I said at the same time. It was our favorite.

After waiting in a long line, it was finally our turn. My mom and I climbed in, but my dad decided take pictures

from behind the gate. He hated the sinking feeling you get in your stomach . . . but I loved it! After that, my mom and I moved onto the Viking, the raft ride, and bumper cars.

After going on every single ride twice, it was finally game time.

And here's the thing: You know how in some families the parents are nice and sometimes let their kids win? Well, I guess being a superhero makes you really competitive, because my parents want to win just as much as I do!

We played all the games, and by the time we were done, Mom had won a medium-size dolphin, Dad had a tiny fish, and I had a teddy bear that was bigger than me!

And I swear, I didn't use any superpowers to win.

We grabbed some hot dogs and popcorn for a late lunch, and I set my teddy bear down next to me while I ate.

"Are you still feeling down, Mia?" asked Mom.

"Nope," I said. "This vacation is really working out."

"Great, and guess what? We still have time today," said Dad. "If you wanted, we could go back to the beach."

I thought about it carefully.

As I've told you, I've been scared about a lot of stuff in my life. And up until now, I've faced my fears to get over them and tackled unexpected situations head-on. So I decided that this was that kind of moment. There was no reason to avoid going back to the beach because of what happened yesterday.

So we dropped our stuff at the hotel and then headed back down to the beach. It was time for a beach redo!

CHAPTER 8

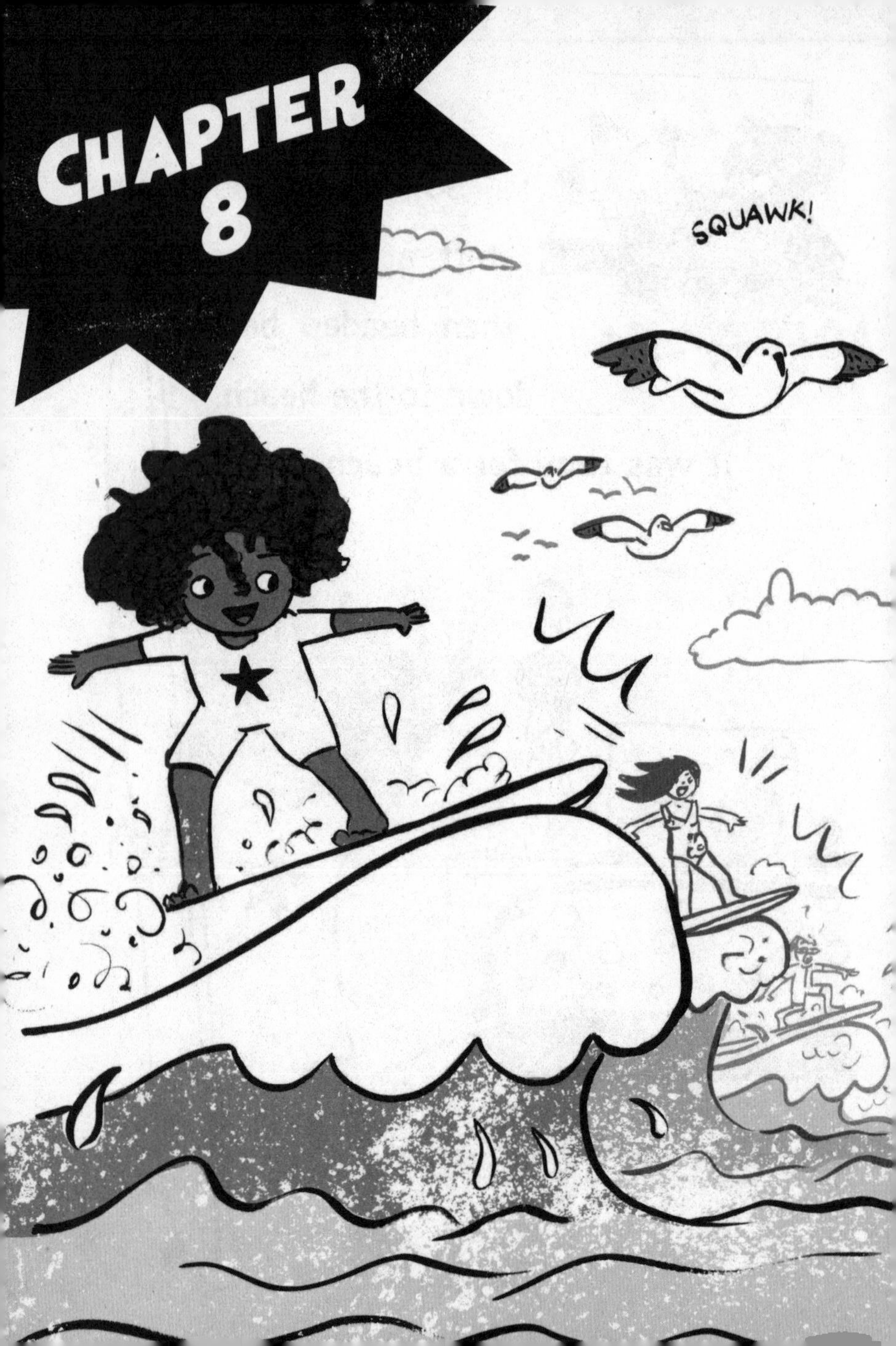

A NEW FRIEND

This time, when my family and I got to the beach, all three of us hit the surf. The water was great, and there was one perfect wave after another! Every time I caught a wave, I imagined I was flying . . . and it worked! My balance was definitely getting better.

Just then, Dad called out, "Hey, watch this!"

He was standing on his surfboard, riding the wave in—and there were fish jumping in circles over the board! It almost looked like my dad and the fish were performing together.

"I don't think I'll ever be that good at surfing," I said with awe.

"Sure you will," said Mom. "He wasn't always that good, you know."

"He wasn't?" I asked.

"Nope. In fact, he started getting better when he was teaching you! One way to get better at something is to teach somebody else."

"Yeah, I guess you're right," I replied.

As I watched Dad's next trick, I promised myself that I would practice a *lot*.

Maybe by our next vacation, I could do a few tricks of my own!

After practicing and falling a lot more, I decided I needed a break, so I left the water and went back to our umbrella.

That's when I saw someone walking toward me. It was the girl whose sandcastle I ruined!

I started to get really nervous, and I could feel a big lump in my throat. Was she going to yell at me? Maybe I could just run back into the ocean. Or be really still and pretend to be a crab.

But before I could think of an escape plan, she was right in front of me.

Oh boy. Here we go again.

"Hi," she said. "I'm Patrice."

"Hi, I'm Mia," I said, with a deep breath.

"I, um . . ." She paused and then looked back at where her family was. "I came over to apologize," she said.

Wait, hold on. Did you hear that?

Why was she sorry?

I was so shocked that you probably could have knocked me over with a seagull feather.

"If anyone should apologize, it should be me," I said. "I'm the one who started it all. The birds were following me, and I went over to your sandcastle."

"But there's something you don't know," she said quietly. "I hid some juice boxes in the sandcastle. For pretend treasure, you know? Somehow the seagulls knew they were there. But I was too embarrassed to tell the truth."

I couldn't believe it. The seagulls were just doing what they were told! They just didn't know that the hidden juice boxes weren't trash!

Right away, I felt like the lump in my throat was gone.

It wasn't totally my fault after all!

"Thanks for telling me," I said. "But I'm sorry too. It was such a cool castle!"

"Thanks, but since I have to start over anyway"—she paused—"want to help me?"

I smiled big and nodded.

The one thing I hadn't done yet on this vacation was build a sandcastle, and there was no time to waste!

SAND SCULPTURES

We had just met, but Patrice and I made a great team. I couldn't believe it!

We filled up our buckets and then took them to the water to wet the sand. Then we measured and drew out what we were going to build.

The main castle was done in no time. After that, we focused on all the other places in the kingdom.

There was a small castle for the village shoemaker, a castle-shaped bookstore, and even a veterinarian's office!

We built everything on our own, but we had some unexpected help, too!

The seagulls must've felt bad about yesterday because they brought over beautiful pieces of seaweed for us to use as decoration.

"I still don't understand how the seagulls seem to know us," Patrice said, confused.

I just smiled and shrugged. I knew how, but I couldn't spoil my super-secret.

When we ran out of buildings to make, we decided to move on to our next project.

"What should we do next?" I asked.

Patrice held up a shovel. "I've got a plan. It involves two very big holes and both our dads!"

I smiled big. It was a perfect plan!

So we began to dig, dig, and dig some more. As I wiped away sweat, I kind of wished I could use my superspeed to dig my hole.

But when Patrice looked over and gave me a high five, I realized that sometimes it's nice to do things the old-fashioned way. Especially with a new friend!

When we were finally knee-deep, we called our dads over and made each of them lie down in a hole.

"Just relax," I said, smiling at Patrice. "We'll take care of the rest!"

We covered them up, and then, using our shovels, we carefully shaped the sand around them. By the time we were done, Patrice's dad was a merman,

and my dad was inside a shark's mouth!
And thanks to the seagulls, they were
perfectly decorated with pretty shells
and seaweed too.

As I admired our work, I spotted the same lifeguard from yesterday walking over.

Oh no, were we doing something wrong again?

Were the holes too big?

Did we use too much sand?

Did we break something by mistake?

Just as I was about to break everything down, she looked at our dads and smiled.

"Hey, girls! Hope you're having fun!" she cried as she turned to look at me. "We saw how much work you did to clean up our beach. You made it cleaner and safer for everybody here—including the wildlife! And as a thank-you, I wanted to give you these."

Then she handed me something.

FOR YOU!

When I looked closer, it was a coupon for free ice cream, and a roll of tickets for rides at the beach carnival . . . for me *and* a friend!

THE PERFECT VACATION

This was the bestest surprise ever! I was worried I'd done more harm than good, but these tickets proved me wrong.

Patrice and I were excited to enjoy dessert, so my family and Patrice and her dad headed to the boardwalk.

I got chocolate ice cream with gummy bears, while Patrice picked her three favorite flavors.

"Wait!" I said before she started eating. "We have to make a toast."

So we held up our cones, and I said, "To the awesomest sandcastle kingdom in the world, new friends, and very nice lifeguards!"

"Yes, and to the best vacation ever!" she added.

Then we gently bumped our cones and took a bite. Mine was delicious, and I could tell hers was too.

It had a bumpy start, but I had to agree—this really was the best vacation ever. I knew that cleaning up the beach was the right thing to do, and in the end it paid off. Not only did I get free ice cream, but I got a new friend, too!

"Man, I wish tomorrow wasn't the last day of vacation," I said with a groan as I licked the ice cream off my fingers.

"Don't worry—there's plenty of time before tomorrow," Patrice said, pointing at the Ferris wheel. "We still need to ride that!"

I looked up at the sky.

The gigantic wheel was lit up in pretty neon colors.

"You're totally right! Come on, let's go!" I cheered.

I love fast roller coasters, but nothing is better than sitting at the top of the Ferris wheel.

As we looked out in front of us, it felt like we had all the time in the world.

And that's when it hit me: When everything went wrong, I didn't know what to do because I couldn't use my powers. I couldn't be superfast, or be superstrong, or even be superbrave.

But here's what this trip taught me: You don't have to be an actual superhero to be a hero—sometimes being a hero is being responsible for yourself and doing the right thing. Whether that's taking care of your beach, your neighborhood, or your school.

I'd been so focused on my superpower skills lately that I forgot about all the super things I can do as regular Mia Macarooney.

And I felt great about that!

After we got off the Ferris wheel the second time, my mom and dad gave me a big hug.

I was bummed that our epic family vacation was almost over. Soon, we'd be back in our normal routine, and I'd be as busy as ever.

But for now, there was nowhere I'd rather be. For tonight, I was going to slow down, take a breath, and enjoy every last second of this vacation . . . as regular me.